igloobooks

Published in 2013
by Igloo Books Ltd
Cottage Farm
Sywell
NN6 0BJ
www.igloobooks.com

FIR003 1013
8 10 12 11 9 7
ISBN: 978-0-85780-426-6

Printed and manufactured in China

Bear's Magic Moon

igloobooks

Little Polar Bear's home is cold and snowy.
The icebergs glimmer... the water sparkles...

...and Little Polar Bear plays with her friends all day long.

She loves rolling in the crisp, white snow until her fur sparkles.
She loves diving into the blue, swirly water and chasing fish.

There's just one thing that Little Polar Bear doesn't like.

The night is very, very...

...DARK!

All the polar bears are gathering to welcome the full moon.
Tonight is a very special night.

"Come with me, Little Polar Bear,"
says Daddy. "It will be great fun."

"We will sing songs.

We will dance until the sun
rises over the icebergs.

We will dive in the water
and chase the sleepy seals.
And the Wise Old Bear will tell us about his adventures."

But Little Polar Bear is so scared of the dark that Daddy
goes to welcome the new moon by himself.

"I'll never be able to welcome the new moon," says Little Polar Bear. "I'm just not brave enough."

Big tears roll down her nose and plop onto the ice.

Then, she hears a heavy paw-step, scrunching in the snow.
Little Polar Bear is very scared!

But, it's only the Wise Old Bear!
"Don't cry, Little Polar Bear," he says.
"There's nothing to be afraid of.
Come outside and you will see something wonderful."

Little Polar Bear shivers and shakes,
but she goes outside with the Wise Old Bear.

Little Polar Bear is frightened.

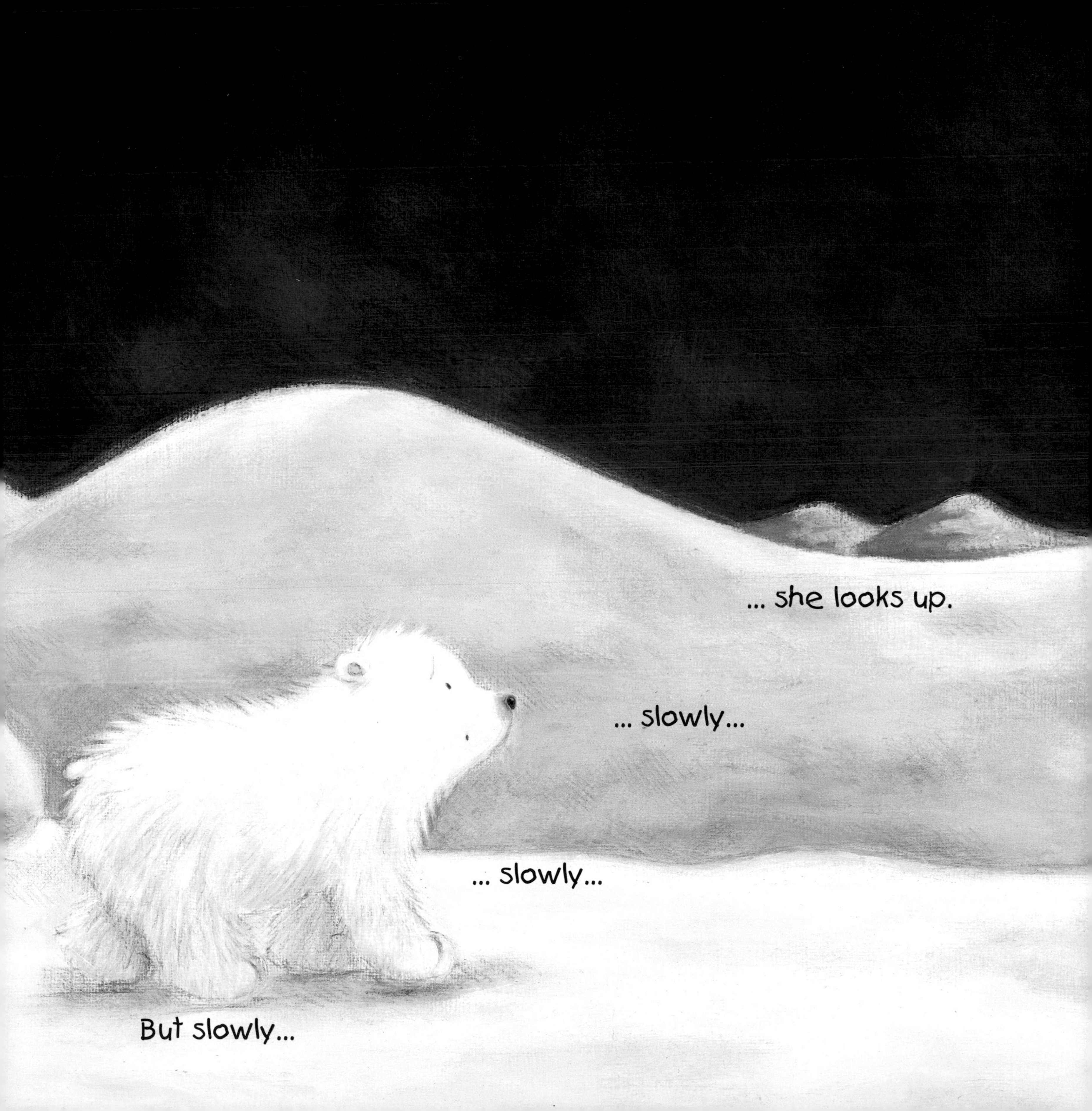

But slowly...

... slowly...

... slowly...

... she looks up.

The round moon is full and bright.
"It's so beautiful," whispers Little Polar Bear.

"The moon and the stars are your friends," says the Wise Old Bear.
"You can tell them all your secrets.
They have watched over bears for hundreds and
hundreds of years and they will watch over you, too."

Little Polar Bear runs to meet Daddy.

"You're here!" he says.

They jump and dive and play in the water.

They sing and dance in the moonlight.

Daddy gives Little Polar Bear a big bear hug.

"You did something very special," he says.

"You did something even though you were scared.

Do you know what that makes you, Little Polar Bear?"

"The bravest bear of all!"

"Goodbye, see you soon!"